# The Twelve Dancing Princesses

## and other princess stories

Compiled by Tig Thomas

Miles
KeLLY

First published in 2013 by Miles Kelly Publishing Ltd
Harding's Barn, Bardfield End Green, Thaxted, Essex, CM6 3PX, UK

2 4 6 8 10 9 7 5 3 1

Publishing Director  Belinda Gallagher
Creative Director  Jo Cowan
Editorial Director  Rosie McGuire
Senior Editor  Claire Philip
Senior Designer  Joe Jones
Production Manager  Elizabeth Collins
Reprographics  Stephan Davis, Jennifer Hunt, Thom Allaway

ISBN 978-1-78209-216-2

Printed in China

British Library Cataloguing-in-Publication Data
A catalogue record for this book is available from the British Library

ACKNOWLEDGEMENTS
The publishers would like to thank the following artists who have contributed to this book:
Smiljana Coh, Marcin Piwowarski, Mélanie Florian (inc. cover)

All other artwork from the Miles Kelly Artwork Bank

The publishers would like to thank the following sources for the use of their photographs:
Cover frame: Karina Bakalyan/Shutterstock.com
Inside frame: asmjp/Shutterstock.com

Made with paper from a sustainable forest
www.mileskelly.net   info@mileskelly.net

# Contents

# Admetus and Alcestis

By James Baldwin

THE KING OF IOLCUS was a cruel tyrant named Pelias, who cared for nobody but himself. Pelias had a daughter named Alcestis, who was as fair as a rose, and so gentle and good that everybody praised her. Many a prince from over the sea had come to woo Alcestis but there was only one to whom she would listen — her handsome young neighbour, King Admetus.

So Admetus went before King Pelias to ask him whether he might marry Alcestis.

"If you want her," said the cruel king "you must come for her in a chariot drawn by a lion and a wild boar." And Pelias laughed, and drove the young man out of his palace.

Admetus went away feeling very sad, for who had ever heard of harnessing a lion and a wild boar together in a chariot? It seemed absolutely impossible.

Early the next morning he built an altar of stones in the open field and lifted his hands towards the mountain tops and called to the god Apollo.

"Lord of the Silver Bow," he cried, "if ever I have shown kindness to the distressed, come now and help me, for I am in need."

Hardly was he done speaking when the bright god Apollo came down and stood before him.

"Kindest of kings," he said, "tell me how I can help you."

Then Admetus told him all about the fair Alcestis, and the harsh condition her father had made.

"Come with me," said Apollo, "and I will help you."

The two went together into the forest, Apollo leading the way. Soon they chased a lion from its lair and the quick-footed Apollo seized the beast by its mane, and although it howled and snapped with its fierce jaws he slipped a bridle upon it. Then Admetus scared a wild boar from a thicket.

When Apollo had caught that too, he went on through the forest, leading the two beasts, one with his right hand, the other with his left. A golden chariot stood by the roadside as if waiting for them, and the lion

and the boar were soon
harnessed to it. It was a strange
team, and the two beasts tried hard
to fight each other, but Apollo lashed
them with a whip until they lost their
fierceness and obeyed him.

Admetus climbed into the chariot,
Apollo stood by his side and held the reins
and drove into Iolcus.

King Pelias was astonished when he saw
the wonderful chariot
and the glorious
charioteer, and

when Admetus again asked him for the Princess Alcestis, he could not refuse.

And so Admetus and Alcestis were married, and everybody except gruff King Pelias was glad. Apollo himself was a guest at the wedding feast, and he brought a present for the young bridegroom, it was a promise from the Mighty Folk upon the mountain top that if Admetus should ever be sick and in danger of death, he might become well again if someone who loved him would die for him.

Admetus and Alcestis lived together happily for a long time, and all the people in their little kingdom loved and blessed them. But at last Admetus fell sick, and, as he grew worse, all feared he would die. Then those who loved him remembered the wedding gift that Apollo had given him, and they began to ask who would be willing to die for him.

His brothers and sisters were asked if they would die for Admetus, but they turned away. There were men in the town whom he had befriended and who owed their lives to him, but they too refused to help.

Now, while everyone was shaking their heads and saying, "Not I," Alcestis went into her room and called to Apollo. She asked if she might give up her life to save her husband. Then without a thought of fear she lay down upon her bed and closed her eyes, and when her maidens came into the room they found her dead.

At the very same time Admetus felt his sickness leave him, and he sprang up as well and strong as he had ever been. He made haste to find his beloved Alcestis and tell her the good news. But when he went into her room, he found her lying lifeless on her couch, and knew at once that she had died for him. His grief was so great that he could not speak, and he wished that death had taken him instead.

Throughout the land every eye was wet with weeping for Alcestis. Admetus sat by the couch where his young queen lay, and held her cold hand in his own. All through the dark hours he sat there alone. The morning dawned, but he did not want to see the light.

At last the sun began to rise in the east, and then Admetus was surprised to feel the hand that he held growing warm. He saw a pink tinge coming into the pale cheeks of Alcestis. A moment later she opened her eyes and sat up, alive and well.

# Admetus and Alcestis

As Admetus held Alcestis' hand, he told her he was overjoyed to be reunited with her again.

When Alcestis had died, the Shadow

Leader led her to Proserpine, the queen of the Underworld.

"Who is this who comes so willingly?" asked the pale-faced queen.

And when she was told how Alcestis had given her life to save her husband, she was moved with pity. Proserpine told the Shadow Leader take Alcestis back to the sunlight of the Upperworld.

So Alcestis came back to life, and for many years she and Admetus lived happily in their kingdom. At last, when they were very old, the Shadow Leader led them both away together.

# The Ruby Prince

By Flora Annie Steel

THERE WAS ONCE an Indian king who was given a snake-stone, just like a ruby, red and fiery. The king called his queen, and gave the jewel to her for safe-keeping. The queen wrapped it in cotton wool and put it away in an empty chest, locking the chest with double locks.

So there the ruby snake-stone lay for twelve long years. At the end of that time the king sent for his queen, and said, "Bring me the ruby, I want to check that it is safe."

The queen told her servant to bring the box, and they unlocked the chest. To everybody's astonishment out stepped a handsome young man.

"Who are you?" said the king, "and where is my jewel?"

"I am the Ruby Prince," said the man, "More than that you cannot know."

The king had a fair daughter, who fell in love with the young man. They were married in great state, and half the kingdom was given to them to rule.

But the young bride, as much as she loved her handsome husband, was sad because she didn't know who he was. The other women in the palace teased her for marrying a complete stranger.

So day after day, she would ask her husband to tell her who he was, and every day the Ruby Prince would reply, "Dear heart, that you must not know!"

Yet still the princess begged and wept, until one day when they were standing by the riverside, she whispered, "If you love me, tell me where you come from!"

Now the Ruby Prince's foot touched the water as he replied, "Dear heart, that you must not know!"

But the princess said again, "If you love me, tell me where you are from!"

The Ruby Prince stood knee-deep in the water. His face was sad as he replied, "Dear heart, that you must not know!"

Again the bride asked her question. By this time the Ruby Prince was up to his waist in the stream.

"Dear heart, anything but that!" He cried.

"Tell me!" cried the princess, and as she

spoke, a jewelled snake wearing a crown reared out of the water. It had a ruby in the middle of its forehead. Then with a sorrowful look, the snake disappeared beneath the surface.

Then the princess went home and wept bitterly, cursing her own curiosity. She wished she hadn't asked her husband to tell her where he had come from. The princess offered a reward of a bushel of gold to anyone who could bring her any information about her husband.

At last a dancing-woman came to the princess and said, "Last night when I was out gathering sticks, I lay down to rest under a tree, and fell asleep. When I awoke it was light, but neither daylight nor moonlight. While I wondered, a sweeper came out from a snake-hole at the foot of the tree, and swept the ground with his broom. Then followed two carpet-bearers, who spread costly rugs, and then disappeared. Then I heard music, and from the snake-hole came a procession of young men, glittering with jewels, and the middle one seemed to be the king.

"While the musicians played, one by one the young men rose and danced. But one, who wore a red ruby on his forehead, danced poorly and looked pale and sad."

The princess recognized the description of her husband, so the next night she went with the dancing-girl to the tree, where they hid and waited to see what might happen.

Sure enough, after a while it became light that was neither sunlight nor moonlight. Then just as the dancing-woman had described, the glittering procession swept out. How the princess's heart ached when she saw how pale her husband had become.

When all had performed before the king, the light faded, and the princess crept home. Every night she would go to the tree and watch, but all day she would weep, because she couldn't figure out how to get her husband back.

Then one day the dancing-girl came to the princess and said, "O princess, I think I have hit upon a plan. The snake-king is passionately fond of dancing, and yet it is only men who dance before him. Now, what if a woman were to dance in front of him instead? He might be so pleased that he would grant her anything she asked for?"

So the princess learnt to dance, and in an incredibly short time she was far better than her teacher. Never before or since was such a graceful, charming, elegant dancer seen. Everything about her was perfection. Then she dressed herself in the finest jewelled muslins and brocades, till she shone and sparkled like a star.

That night, with a fast-beating heart she nervously hid behind the tree and waited. When they appeared, as before, the Ruby Prince looked paler and sadder than ever, and when his turn came to dance, he hesitated, as if sick at heart.

But from behind the tree stepped the princess, and she danced marvellously before the king. Never before was there such a dance! Everybody held their breath till it was done, and then the king cried aloud, "O unknown dancer, ask for whatever you like, and it shall be yours!"

"Please give me the man who looks so sad, for that is why I danced!" replied the princess at once.

The snake-king looked very fierce, and his eyes glittered as he said, "I would kill you were it not for my promise. Take him, and be gone!"

Quick as a thought, the princess seized the Ruby Prince by the hand, dragged him beyond the circle, and fled.

After that they lived very happily. The princess held her tongue and never again asked her husband where he came from.

# The Twelve Dancing Princesses

By the Brothers Grimm

ONCE UPON A TIME there was a king who had twelve daughters, each one more beautiful than the other. Their beds were all together in one room, and when they went to bed, their door was locked and barred. But the next morning their shoes were always danced to pieces, and no one knew where they had been or how it had happened.

The king proclaimed that whoever could

discover where the princesses went dancing each night could choose one of them for his wife and become king after his death.

Now it happened that a poor soldier, who because of his wounds could no longer serve in the army, was making his way to the city where the king lived. He met an old woman who asked him where he was going. "I'm not sure myself," he said. "But I would like to become king and discover where the princesses are dancing their shoes to pieces."

"Oh," said the old woman, "that isn't so difficult. Just do not drink the wine that one of them will bring you in the evening." Then she gave him a cloak and said, "Put this on, and you will be invisible, and you can follow them."

Having received this good advice, the

soldier went to the king, and announced himself as a suitor. He was well received, and was given royal clothes to wear.

That evening at bedtime he was escorted to a bedchamber outside the princesses' room. Just as he was going to bed, the eldest princess brought him a goblet of wine, but he secretly poured it away. He lay down, and after a little while began to snore as if he were in the deepest sleep. The twelve princesses heard him and laughed.

Then they got up, opened their wardrobes, chests, and closets, took out their best clothes, and made themselves beautiful in front of their mirrors.

When they were ready, they approached the soldier, but he did not move at all as he feigned sleep. As soon as they thought it was safe, the eldest princess went to her bed and knocked on it. It immediately sank beneath the floor, revealing a trapdoor.

The soldier watched how they all climbed down, one after the other, the eldest leading the way. When the youngest princess had gone through, he jumped up, put on the cloak, and followed her. But halfway down the stairs he accidentally stepped on her dress. Frightened, she called out, "It's not right! Something is holding my dress."

"Don't be so silly," said the eldest princess. "You have just caught yourself on a hook."

Then they passed through three walkways lined with trees made from gold, then silver, then clear diamond. The soldier broke a twig from each. The cracking sound frightened the youngest princess each time, but the eldest princess insisted that it was only the sounds of joyful salutes.

They continued until they came to a large lake. Twelve boats were there, and in each boat there was a handsome prince waiting for them. Each prince took a princess into his boat. The soldier snuck into the boat of the youngest princess, and her prince said at once, "I am as strong as ever, but the boat seems to be much heavier. I am rowing as hard as I can."

On the other side of the water there was a beautiful, brightly illuminated castle. Joyful music, kettle drums, and trumpets sounded forth. They rowed over and went inside.

Each handsome prince danced with his

princess. The soldier danced along as well, and when a princess held up a goblet of wine, he drank it empty as she lifted it to her mouth. This frightened the youngest princess, but the eldest silenced her every time. They danced there until three o'clock the next morning, when their shoes were worn to pieces.

The princes rowed them back across the water. When they were on the steps, the soldier ran ahead and got into bed so that when the twelve tired princesses came in he was again snoring loudly.

"He will be no risk to us," they said. Then they took off their beautiful clothes, put them away, placed their worn out shoes under their beds and went to sleep.

The next morning the soldier said nothing, for he wanted to see the amazing thing again. He went along the second and third nights, and everything happened as before. Each time they danced until their shoes were in pieces. The third time he also took a goblet as a piece of evidence.

Eventually the hour came when he was to give his answer. He brought the three twigs and the goblet with him. The twelve princesses stood behind the door and listened to what he had to say. The king asked, "So, where did my daughters go at night to dance their shoes to pieces?"

He answered easily, "In an underground castle with twelve princes." Then he told the whole story and brought forth the pieces of evidence. When the princesses saw that they had been found out, and that their denials did no good, they admitted everything.

Then the king asked the soldier which princess he would like for a wife. He answered, "I myself am no longer young, so I'd like to marry the eldest princess."

Their wedding was held the very same day, and the kingdom was promised to him following the king's death.

# Tatterhood

By George Webbe Dasent

ONCE UPON A TIME there was a king and queen who had two baby princesses. The first to be born had a wooden spoon in her hand, and rode upon a goat.

"If I'm your mamma," said the queen, "Then God give me grace to do better next time."

"Oh, don't be sorry," said the girl, who rode on the goat, "for one will soon come after me who is better looking."

After a while the queen had another girl,

who was so fair and sweet, no one had ever set eyes on such a lovely child. They called the eldest girl Tatterhood, because she was always so plain, and because she wore a hood that hung about her ears in tatters.

One Christmas Eve, when the princesses were grown-up, there rose a frightful noise outside the queen's chamber. Tatterhood asked what it was that crashed so loudly.

The queen told her that a pack of witches had turned up. So Tatterhood said she would go out and drive them away. She begged the queen to be mindful and keep all the doors closed. Having said this, off she went with her wooden spoon. She began to hunt and sweep away the hags. While this was happening there was such a loud noise in the passage.

Now, exactly what happened next I'm

sure I can't tell, but Tatterhood's sister had just peeped out to see how things were going when POP, up came an old witch, who whisked her out of the window. When Tatterhood came back and found her sister gone, she scolded everyone nearby for not taking better care.

"I'll see if I can set her free," she said.

She asked the king for a boat but no captain or sailors. She would sail away all

alone. As there was no stopping her, at last they let her have her own way. So Tatterhood sailed off, and steered her boat to where the witches lived.

When she came to the landing-place, she rode on her goat up to the witches' castle. Tatterhood saw her sister weeping through an open window, so she leapt on her goat, jumped inside, snatched up her sister, and they set off.

The witches came after her, trying to get the princess back again. They flocked about her as thick as a swarm of bees. But the goat snorted and butted with his horns, and Tatterhood beat and banged them with her wooden spoon, and the pack of witches had to give up.

They set off for home but the winds blew strongly and their boat was blown into a strange land. The king of that land had two sons. When he saw the strange sail, he sent messengers down to the beach to find out where it came from, and who owned it.

When the king's men arrived there, they saw not a living soul on board but Tatterhood, and there she was, riding round and round the deck on her goat at full speed, till her straggly hair streamed in the wind. The folk from the palace were all amazed, and asked if there was anyone else on board?

"Yes," said Tatterhood, "my sister."

They wanted to see her but Tatterhood said, "No one shall see her, unless the king comes himself."

When the servants got back to the palace and told what they had seen, the king and his sons set out at once. When they got there, Tatterhood led out her fair sister. The king's eldest son fell in love straight away and asked to marry her. Tatterhood said he couldn't, unless the youngest son chose to marry Tatterhood as well. The younger prince wasn't keen, but at last the king talked him round.

When all was ready, they were to go to church. The younger prince thought it was the saddest day of his life. First, the older prince drove off with his bride, and she was so lovely that all the people stopped to look at her. Next came the sorrowful younger prince on horseback by the side of Tatterhood, who trotted along on her goat with her wooden spoon.

"Why don't you talk?" asked Tatterhood.

"What should I talk about?" answered the youngest prince.

"Well, you might at least ask me why I ride upon this ugly goat," said Tatterhood.

"Why do you ride on that ugly goat?" asked the prince.

"Is it an ugly goat? Why, it's the grandest horse a bride ever rode on," answered Tatterhood, and in a trice the goat became the finest horse the prince had ever seen.

Then they rode on again, but the prince didn't say a word. So Tatterhood asked him again why he didn't talk, and said, "You can at least ask me why I ride with this ugly spoon in my fist."

"Why do you ride with that ugly spoon?" asked the prince.

"Is it an ugly spoon? Why, it's the loveliest silver wand a bride ever bore," said Tatterhood, and in a trice it became a silver wand, so dazzling bright, that sunbeams glistened from it.

So they rode on a bit further, but the prince was just as sorrowful, and never said a word. In a little while, Tatterhood told him to ask why she wore the ugly grey hood. So he asked and she said, "Is it an ugly hood? Why, it's the brightest crown a bride ever wore." And it became a golden crown on the spot.

Now, they rode on a long while again, and the prince was so woeful, that he sat without sound or speech just as before. So his bride asked him again why he didn't talk, and told him to ask, why her face was so ugly and ashen-grey?

"Ah!" asked the prince, "why is your face so ugly and ashen-grey?"

"I, ugly?" said the bride. "You think my sister pretty, but I am ten times prettier."

And lo, when the prince looked at her, she was so lovely, he thought there was never so lovely a woman in all the world. After that, I shouldn't wonder if the prince found his tongue, and no longer rode along with his head hanging down.

So they drank both deep and long from the bridal cup, and after that both princes set out with their brides to the princesses' father's palace, and there they had another grand feast.

And, if you make haste and run, I dare
say you'll find there's still a drop of the
bridal ale left for you.